TANA HOBAN
Exactly the Opposite

Greenwillow Books

An Imprint of HarperCollinsPublishers

The full-color photographs
were reproduced
from 35-mm. slides.

Manufactured in China.
by South China Printing
Company Ltd.
For information address
HarperCollins Children's
Books, a division of
HarperCollins Publishers,
10 East 53rd Street,
New York, NY 10022.
www.harperchildrens.com

First Edition
10 11 12 13 SCP 10 9

Library of Congress
Cataloging-in-Publication Data
Hoban, Tana.
Exactly the opposite/
Tana Hoban.
     p.   cm.
"Greenwillow Books."
Summary: Photographs of
familiar outdoor scenes
illustrate pairs of opposites.
ISBN 0-688-08861-9.
ISBN 0-688-08862-7 (lib. bdg.)
ISBN 0-688-15473-5 (pbk.)
1. English language—
Synonyms and antonyms—
Juvenile literature.
[1. English language—
Synonyms and antonyms.]
I. Title.
PE1591.H58   1990
428.1—dc20
89-27227   CIP   AC

This one is for Gail